characters created by

lauren child

I want to be much more bigger like you

Grosset & Dunlap

Charlie and Lola™

Text based on the script written by Carol Noble

Illustrations from the TV animation produced by Tiger Aspect

GROSSET & DUNLAP
Published by the Penguin Group
Penguin Group (USA) Inc., 375 Hudson Street, New York, New York 10014, USA
Penguin Group (Canada), 90 Eglinton Avenue East, Suite 700, Toronto, Ontario M4P 2Y3, Canada
(a division of Pearson Penguin Canada Inc.)
Penguin Books Ltd., 80 Strand, London WC2R 0RL, England
Penguin Group Ireland, 25 St. Stephen's Green, Dublin 2, Ireland
(a division of Penguin Books Ltd.)
Penguin Group (Australia), 250 Camberwell Road, Camberwell, Victoria 3124, Australia
(a division of Pearson Australia Group Pty. Ltd.)
Penguin Books India Pvt. Ltd., 11 Community Centre, Panchsheel Park, New Delhi—110 017, India
Penguin Group (NZ), 67 Apollo Drive, Rosedale, North Shore 0632, New Zealand
(a division of Pearson New Zealand Ltd.)
Penguin Books (South Africa) (Pty.) Ltd., 24 Sturdee Avenue,
Rosebank, Johannesburg 2196, South Africa

Penguin Books Ltd., Registered Offices: 80 Strand, London WC2R 0RL, England

Library of Congress Cataloging-in-Publication Data is available.

ISBN 978-0-448-44867-1   10 9 8 7 6 5 4 3 2 1

I have this little sister, Lola.
She is small and very funny.
  Lola says, "I'm not small, Charlie.
I am getting more **bigger**
    and grown-up all of the time."

"And now that I am
much more **bigger**,
I can go on the
Super Duper
Loopy Loopy ride."

So I say,
"The **Super Dooper**
Loop the **Looper** is
very, **very** SCARY.
Are you sure?"

"I am **very** sure, Charlie,"
says Lola.

So I measure Lola
to see if she really is
bigger.

"Charlie, I must be
more **taller** than that!
Are you **tricking** me?"

"No, Lola. That's exactly
how **big** you are."

Then Lola says,
"But, I absolutely MUST
be **big** enough to
go on the **Super Duper
Loopy Loopy** ride."

I say, "There are still
loads of **fun rides**
          at the fair for
smaller people.
          The **Chug-a-Bugs**
ride is really exciting."

And Lola says,
"I **don't** think so, Charlie."

Then Lola says,
"I have a GOOD plan.
I am going to
think myself bigger.

Now I am thinking
I am nearly as
big as a sunflower
touching the sun."

"And now I am thinking I am as **big** as one of those extremely

T
A
L
L
E
S
T

buildings."

I say,
"You can't MAKE yourself
bigger, Lola.
It just happens."

Lola says,
        "It's not fair.
Why am I always, always
        the small one?"

So I say,
        "There are great
things about
        being small. Like . . ."

". . . you get **stories**
read to you
every night . . .

and you get loads of
piggybacks."

But Lola says,
"I still really, **really**
would like being
the **biggest**."

When Marv comes over,
he says,
"Are you ready for
the **Super Dooper**
Loop the **Looper**?"

And Lola shouts,
"I am! I am! I am!"

Then Marv whispers,
"She's quite **small** for the ride,
isn't she, Charlie?"

And I say,
"Yup."

At the fair,
Marv says,
"The **Super Dooper
Loop** the **Looper**
is going to be
the best ride!"

"Yes. It will make
our hair stand
on end," I say.

"And our tummies
go all **funny**,"
says Marv.
"I can't wait!
How about you, Lola?"

"Err . . . I can't wait either . . ."

When we get
to the front of the line
Marv says,
"Hold on to your
tummy, Lola!"

But Lola says,
"Err . . . I think
I might be slightly
too small still.

Perhaps it would be
a little more fun
if I went on something
for more slightly
smaller people—
like the
Chug-a-Bugs!"

So we all go on the **Chug-a-Bugs**
and Lola **laughs** and **laughs**.
   She says, "You were right, Charlie!
The **Chug-a-Bugs** IS the very best ride
   in the whole world and the universe."